This book
belongs to:

....

For friends,
old and new.
A.B.

For Erin
and Isla
S.R.

OXFORD
UNIVERSITY PRESS

Great Clarendon Street, Oxford OX2 6DP

Oxford University Press is a department of the University of Oxford.
It furthers the University's objective of excellence in research,
scholarship,
and education by publishing worldwide in

Oxford   New York

Auckland   Cape Town   Dar es Salaam   Hong Kong   Karachi
Kuala Lumpur   Madrid   Melbourne   Mexico City   Nairobi
New Delhi   Shanghai   Taipei   Toronto

With offices in

Argentina   Austria   Brazil   Chile   Czech Republic   France   Greece
Guatemala   Hungary   Italy   Japan   Poland   Portugal   Singapore

South Korea   Switzerland   Thailand   Turkey   Ukraine   Vietnam

Oxford is a registered trade mark of Oxford University Press
in the UK and in certain other countries

Text © Ann Bonwill 2014
Illustrations © Simon Rickerty 2014
Photograph on page 4 © Graeme Shannon/Shutterstock.com

The moral rights of the author/illustrator have been asserted

Database right Oxford University Press (maker)

First published in 2014

British Library Cataloguing in Publication Data available

ISBN: 978-0-19-273500-3 (paperback)

2 4 6 8 10 9 7 5 3 1

Printed in China

Paper used in the production of this book is a natural,
recyclable product made from wood grown in sustainable forests.
The manufacturing process conforms to the environmental
regulations of the country of origin

I totally don't want to play!

featuring Hugo, Bella, and Cressida!

Ann Bonwill &
Simon Rickerty

OXFORD
UNIVERSITY PRESS

Hello, Bella, are you ready to go skating?

Sorry, Hugo, skating slipped my mind. I'm going to the playground with Cressida.

Cressida?

Yes, Cressida. She's my fabulous new friend!

But Bella, we **always** go skating together.

Embrace change, Hugo. Come to the playground with us. It's bound to be fun with Cressida around.

Supremely fun!

Let me know when the fun starts.

Swings! How I love the feel of the wind in my hair . . .

You don't have any hair.
And there's not much wind.

I just need a push.
Bella, can you help?

My
turn
now.
Who's
going
to
push
me?

Sorry, Hugo.
There's a see-saw
over there that's
just perfect for
Cressida and me.

Hmmm. Something's
not quite right.

Very true. Hugo, come and see-saw with me!

See-saws are awesome!
What shall we play next?
Leap-frog?

You mean leap-croc!

Wait for me . . .

Ow! I totally don't want
to play any more.

This playground isn't made for three. I'm going home.

we are three

friends together!